DOPEY LOSES THE DIAMONDS

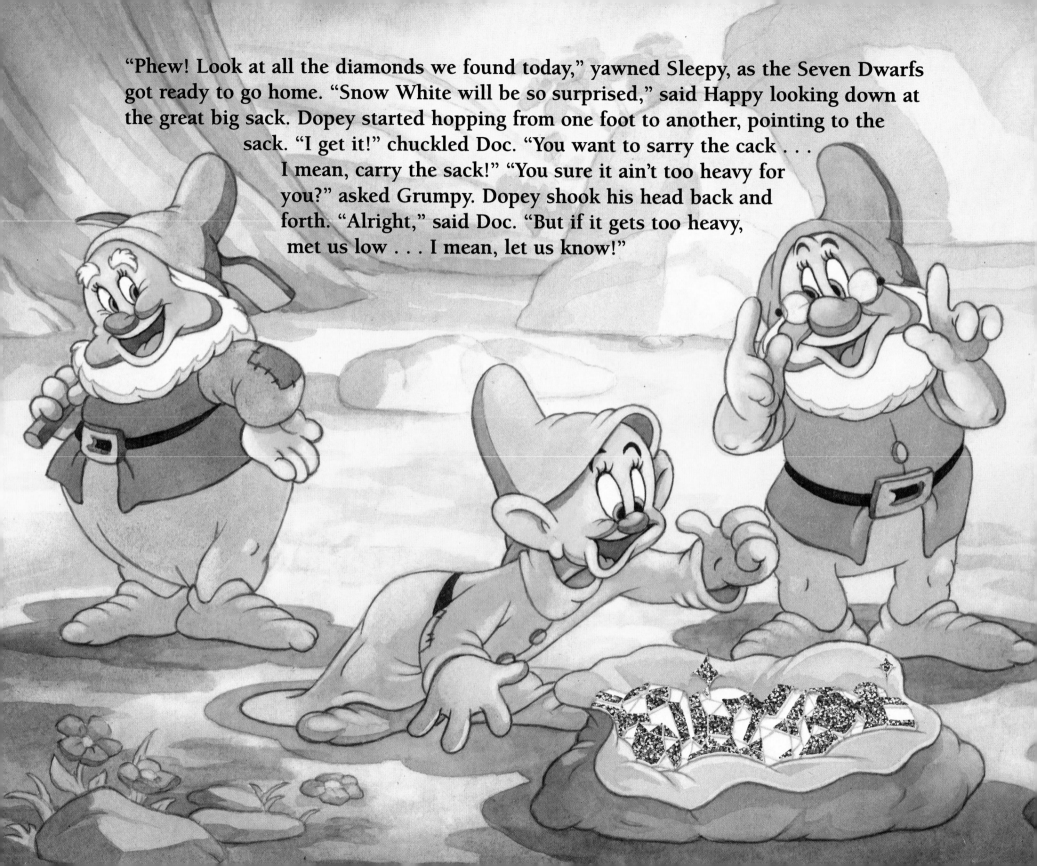

"Phew! Look at all the diamonds we found today," yawned Sleepy, as the Seven Dwarfs got ready to go home. "Snow White will be so surprised," said Happy looking down at the great big sack. Dopey started hopping from one foot to another, pointing to the sack. "I get it!" chuckled Doc. "You want to sarry the cack . . . I mean, carry the sack!" "You sure it ain't too heavy for you?" asked Grumpy. Dopey shook his head back and forth. "Alright," said Doc. "But if it gets too heavy, met us low . . . I mean, let us know!"

Off they marched, singing through the forest. Dopey started out in front, proudly carrying the sack over his shoulder. But that sack was so heavy, poor Dopey got slower and slower. Soon, he was the last dwarf in line. Dopey was tired so he sat down to rest on a log.

As darkness began to fall, Dopey felt scared. When he started toward home again something happened . . . R-i-i-i-pppp! A twig on the log tore a little hole in the sack. Dopey was in such a hurry he didn't notice.

As Dopey ran down the path the sack bounced against his back. With each bounce there was a Rrrip!, as the hole in the sack got bigger and bigger. And with each Rrrip! there was a Plop! Soon, the Plops! turned into Plippety-plops! In no time at all, the Plippety-plops! had become Plippety-plap-pety-plops! But Dopey only noticed that the sack was getting lighter and that meant he could run faster. Dopey liked that.

The little forest animals heard the Plops! and the Plippety-plops! and the Plippety-plappety-plops! very well. One by one, they came out of their nests and burrows and hollow logs to see what was happening. There, sprinkled all along the path, they found hundreds of sparkling diamonds. The raccoons tried to nibble them. The birds pecked at them. The bunnies sniffed them. The squirrels hid them in their cheeks. The deer rolled them around with their noses.

Dopey didn't see what the animals were doing. He just ran and ran. The other dwarfs were at the cottage door with Snow White when Dopey came huffing and puffing across the clearing. "Good for you!" said Doc. "You carried the sack that whole way!" Dopey proudly held the sack out for everyone to see.

Everyone gasped in horror! The sack was empty! "You lost the diamonds! Now our surprise for Snow White is ruined!" snapped Grumpy, grabbing the sack from Dopey. "It's not his fault," Doc said. "The hack had a sole in it . . . I mean the sack had a hole in it!" "Oh dear!" said Snow White. "How will we ever find the diamonds?" They decided to go right out to look for the missing gems. "After all," said Happy. "They'll be right where Dopey dropped them!"

It was a very dark night, so Snow White and the Seven Dwarfs each carried a lantern as they went back along the path. But not one diamond could be found. "I just don't understand it!" muttered Doc to Dopey. "Did you come home along the same path we did?" Dopey sadly nodded, yes. He had let everyone down and he felt awful.

Disappointed, Snow White and the dwarfs returned home. "Look!" said Doc, lifting his lamp up high. All the dwarfs looked. "Omigosh!" exclaimed Happy. "Diamonds are growing in the trees!" "Jumpin' Jewels!" snapped Grumpy. "They're all over the house, too!" "How perfectly lovely," Snow White cheered, as she hurried toward the house. "Who could have done such a thing?" asked all the dwarfs. Then they turned and looked at Dopey. But he was bewildered, too. All Dopey could do was shrug.

Just then there was a rustling in the forest. All the forest animals stepped into the clearing and looked up at the trees. "How sweet!" said Snow White. "The animals decorated the cottage!" It was a wonderful gift for Snow White and the dwarfs. As they all gazed up at the beautiful scene around them, the dwarf who was the happiest of them all was Dopey.

THE END